This Little Tiger book belongs to:

_____

_____

_____

for Ronja Mo
DB

for Becs
EE

LITTLE TIGER PRESS
1 The Coda Centre, 189 Munster Road, London SW6 6AW
www.littletiger.co.uk

First published in Great Britain 2003
This edition published 2004

ISBN 978-1-85430-910-5

A CIP catalogue record for this book is available
from the British Library

Printed in China • LTP/1800/1761/1216

4 6 8 10 9 7 5 3

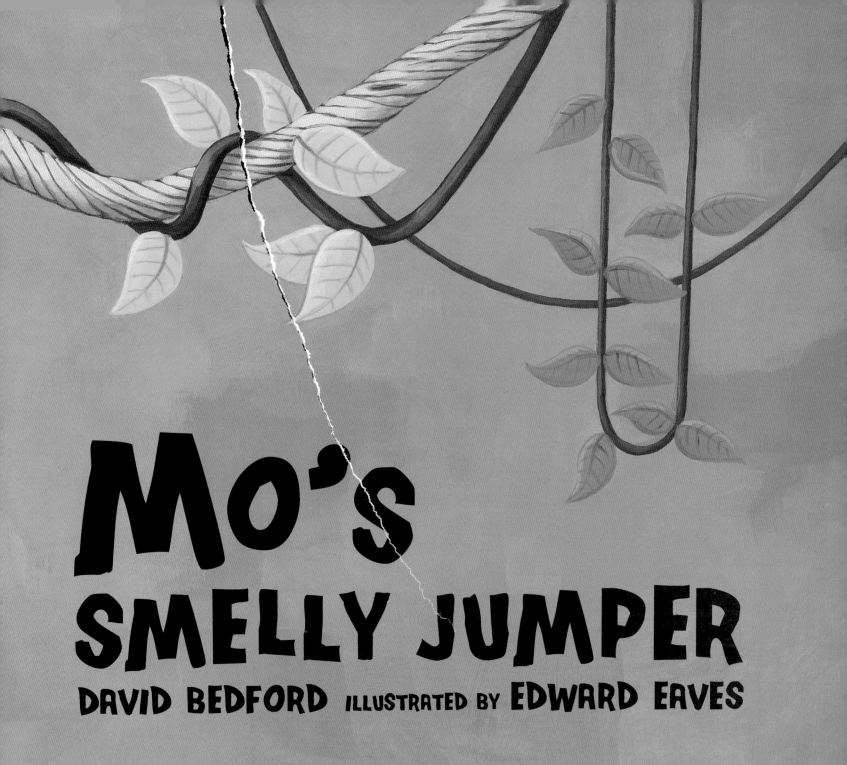

MO'S
SMELLY JUMPER

DAVID BEDFORD ILLUSTRATED BY **EDWARD EAVES**

LITTLE TIGER PRESS
LONDON

Mo Monkey always wore his rainbow jumper.

He wore it when he collected juicy berries
with Mother Monkey . . .

And he wore it when he made
mud pies with his friends, Ellie and Tig.

Mo used his jumper to clean his
hands and feet before dinner . . .

And to wipe his face afterwards.

One day Mother Monkey said, "That jumper is dirty. It smells and pongs and whiffs. I'm going to wash it."

And she pulled the jumper
right over Mo's head!

But Mo wouldn't let go.
Mother Tiger and Tig strolled by.
"Why are you pulling on Mo's
rainbow jumper?" asked Mother Tiger.

"It smells and pongs and whiffs," said Mother Monkey.
"I want to wash it but Mo won't let go. Help me pull."

Mother Tiger helped pull.
But Tig and Mo pulled the other way.
Mother Elephant and Ellie stopped to watch.
"Why is everyone pulling on Mo's rainbow jumper?"
asked Mother Elephant.

"It smells and pongs and whiffs," puffed Mother Monkey.
"I want to wash it but Mo won't let go. Help me pull."

Mother Elephant helped pull.
But Ellie, Tig and Mo pulled the other way.
"Pull!" shouted the mothers.
"Pull!" shouted Ellie, Tig and Mo.

Mo whispered to his friends.
"One, two, three . . .

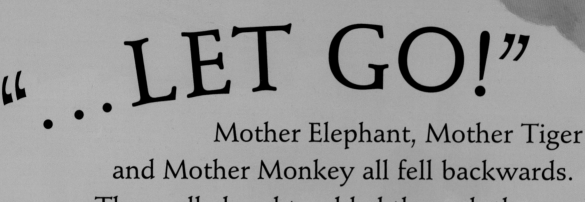

"...LET GO!"

Mother Elephant, Mother Tiger
and Mother Monkey all fell backwards.
They rolled and tumbled through the mud
and landed in a heap. Mo, Ellie and Tig laughed.
"Now *you* all need a wash," giggled Mo.

While the three mothers had a bath, Mo washed the jumper himself until he could see the bright rainbow colours again.

Then he hung it up to dry in the sun.

But when Mo put his jumper back on it hung
all the way down to his feet . . .

"Oh no!" cried Mother Monkey. "We've stretched
your rainbow jumper!"
"Don't worry," said Mo. "My jumper is
even better now because . . .

"… I can *sleep* in it as well!"

More fabulous books from Little Tiger Press!

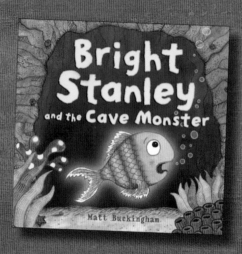

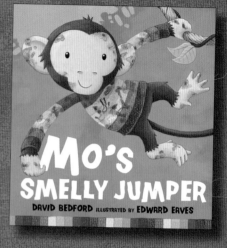

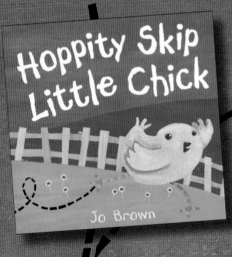

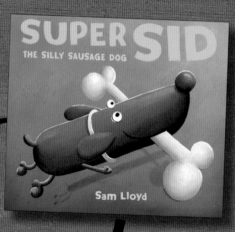

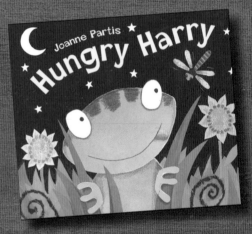

For information regarding any of the above titles
or for our catalogue, please contact us:
Little Tiger Press, 1 The Coda Centre,
189 Munster Road, London SW6 6AW
Tel: 020 7385 6333
E-mail: contact@littletiger.co.uk
www.littletiger.co.uk